CHRISTMAS IN THE EMPTY CABIN

E. REYES

*For Alexander, Isabella, and Eddie Dean.
You three (including your mom) made me like
Christmas and Thanksgiving again.*

VELOX BOOKS
Published by arrangement with the author.

Christmas in the Empty Cabin copyright © 2022 by E. Reyes.

All Rights Reserved.

This book is a work of fiction. People, places, events, and situations are the product of the author's imagination. Any resemblance to actual persons, living or dead, or historical events, is purely coincidental.

No part of this book may be reproduced, stored in a retrieval system, or transmitted by any means without the written permission of the author and publisher.

CONTENTS

Foreword _____ 1

Midnight Visitors _____ 3

My Brother Daniel _____ 11

The House by the Woods _____ 27

Christmas Blues _____ 47

Christmas in the Empty Cabin _____ 49

A Scurry Furry Christmas _____ 67

Afterword _____ 85

About the Author _____ 87

FOREWORD

If you know me, then you know that I am like the Clark Griswald of Halloween. I love it with a passion beyond the movies and the books that cater to October. Halloween didn't feel like it was here this year in the wonderful and surprise-filled year of 2020. It felt like we were already in a horror show—a reality horror show with a lunatic running it, praised by people who gawk at the man with the same fixation and admiration as The Family had with Charles Manson.

And aside from that, the retail and department stores didn't care for Halloween. I'm not sure if people had enough scary things relating to current events or if these stores knew that they wouldn't make money off candies, chocolates, and costumes.

When I'm not writing these stories, I am tirelessly working retail. So, it didn't feel like Halloween or October at all. Thanksgiving and Christmas items replaced the barely stocked Halloween items two weeks into October! So each day, I saw lit Christmas lights, miniature trees, and clothing that didn't pop up until after Halloween. And in the grocery aisles, I would see *Elf* cereal, peppermint coffee creamer, and those sampler packages of cheese and meat.

I was bitter about this situation, but I live for the horror genre and Halloween all year. So, it didn't impact me too negatively. I just wanted to see more things for Halloween.

I remember enjoying Christmas and Thanksgiving very much as a kid when I didn't know shit about the real world or what would happen at home. Once I did know those things, and then bad stuff started happening, I became this Grinch/Scrooge person that didn't care for Christmas.

As an adult, I have and continue to celebrate Christmas as a time for family, reflect on the year, and think about what I want for the next year and tamales—man, do I love beef tamales. And I finally feel that way again, more and more, and I have my family to thank for that.

As I re-edited and polished my stories, I noticed that I had a couple of holiday ones on *Strange Tales of the Macabre* and a short story on an eBook that had never been collected until now. So thus, *Christmas in the Empty Cabin and Other Holiday Tales* was born. I felt like these stories needed a book to be able to breathe and stand out more. And I hope you all enjoy this collection.

Well, my friend, however you celebrate the holidays, I hope you do it responsibly and with others in mind. I wish you and your family a happy holiday. Thank you.

E. Reyes

MIDNIGHT VISITORS

1

It was November 1st, Halloween had just passed, and the holidays were creeping up fast.

It had been a warm autumn day in Devil's Hill, Arizona. It had been a mostly sunny day, but the weather lady—who dressed like a '70s go-go dancer—had predicted heavy rain in the forecast for that night. The dark clouds were already moving in, looking down on Strawberry Avenue. All of the stars were blocked; the moon was obscured. The wind was howling its eerie song as it danced against any physical object it came by. The smell of rain was in the air.

Like most twelve-year-old girls, Sophie couldn't sleep just yet because she was texting her best friend. Sophie was inquiring about a certain boy she had a crush on.

Sophie: Did you see Tyler today? I didn't see him at all.

Sandy: Um… whyyyy???

Sophie: just wondering lol

Sandy: Tyler-Tyler? Tyler, who always has ketchup stains on his shirt? Tyler, who sits by himself during P.E.???

Sophie: Duh, Sandy. Who else?

Sandy: Ewww!!! You like him?! OMG Sophie!

Sophie: What?! He's kinda cute.

Sandy: I'm going to delete these messages and pretend I never read them. My eyes are infected now. I feel sorry for my brain.

Sophie: Oh, stop lol you like Chubby Robbie anyway

Sandy: Not even! I just kissed him on a dare, Sophie! Don't forget that! Lol

Sophie: Trust me, Sandy. I will NEVER forget that lol

Sophie's bedroom door opened, and her mom peeked through, her head tilted to the side. Her mom's light brown hair was hanging down.

"Sophie, phone down, please. I told you already. You have to go to sleep. It's ten p.m.," said her mom.

Sophie rolled her eyes and said, "Ugh, I know, mom. I was asking Sandy exactly when we had to turn in our book report for reading class."

"Honey. That's what you said to your father an *hour* ago. Go to sleep now, okay? You can't be up past midnight," and then solemnly, "especially tonight."

Sophie frowned. "Why not tonight?"

"Sophie," her mother sighed, "don't talk back— just please go to sleep now, okay?"

Weird, thought Sophie.

Sophie let out a sigh. "Okay, okay. Night, mom."

"Goodnight, Honey. Go to sleep."

Sophie texted Sandy that she had to go because "#momproblems." She set the phone down on her nightstand and clicked off the lamp.

Sophie heard the wind howling softly against her window; it sounded like a choir of ghosts singing in a haunted house. The bare trees outside her window were swaying back and forth. The clouds were a light purple and looked fluffy and full of rain.

Sophie couldn't sleep because she was thinking about her mom. Her mom used to be so fun and happy, and energetic. Nowadays, her mom was just a meat suit with no personality. It was as if she was programmed with preset messages and monotone dialogue, except when she became angry. She had become that way since her father died—Sophie's Grandpa Thomas—last year from natural causes. One year prior, Sophie's grandma had already died; they believed Grandpa Thomas had died of a broken heart.

Her mom and Grandpa Thomas were really close; she was his favorite child of the three he had. It made Sophie sad to see her mother so affected by the unfortunate loss of two parents. Sophie's parents sometimes made her mad and depressed, but she couldn't imagine having one die—especially both.

Turning to the wall, Sophie wrapped herself under her warm comforter. She closed her eyes and fell asleep.

2

When Sophie woke up, she thought it was morning already.

"Ohmuhgod, ohmuhgod," she said as she reached for her cell phone. She hit the power key, and the screen lit up. It was indeed the next day, but not quite a sunny morning; it was 12:22 a.m.

Sophie sighed in relief. She set her phone back down, ignoring all her social media notifications, and planned to get much more needed sleep. She felt incredibly tired—drowsy.

Something was tapping at her window.

She looked toward her window. The blinds were slightly opened, and she saw a flash of lightning; rain was tapping against the glass.

For a minute, she was sure it was some kind of monster or alien creature calling her to look. But nope—only rain.

As Sophie turned to face her wall again to drift off to sleep, she heard the front door of her home open and close. Thunder cracked the rainy sky.

Sophie's eyes were open and alert. Her heart started to pump hard in her chest.

Who could that be? She thought. My parents are usually asleep at this time. Dad goes to bed at ten—mom about an hour later. Is someone... breaking in?

Sophie quietly got up from her bed and swiftly drifted to her bedroom door—she locked it. She grabbed her baseball bat—purchased for softball—and retreated to her bed under her comforter. She placed the bat beside her. Her eyes were on the door. She waited for about five more minutes but didn't hear any more noise.

That was too weird, she thought.

After nothing happened and feeling silly for being so scared, Sophie hugged her baseball bat and closed her eyes. Before almost entirely asleep, Sophie started to hear the dishes in the kitchen.

Christmas in the Empty Cabin

Sophie sat in bed and brought the baseball bat out from under the cover. Someone was in her home. She got off her bed and put her ear to the door; she heard dishes and what may have been forks and spoons, knives, and glass cups. She sniffed the air and noticed the sweet and mouthwatering smell of roasted chicken, mashed potatoes, sugar cookies, and other baked goods.

"Why is mom cooking so late?" she pondered.

The rain behind her was still thudding against her window. Lightning was flashing, but no sound of thunder followed.

This is really creeping me out, Sophie thought.

She left her bat in her closet—feeling safe—and decided to go out and have a look.

After slipping on her pink fluffy slippers and matching robe, Sophie unlocked her door and stepped into the hallway. The hallway was dark and cold. She crossed her arms and stopped walking once she gazed into the living room.

There were about a dozen colorful sugar skulls on the coffee table. Day of the Dead ceramic figures of skeletons and crosses were placed between them. Mexican pastries were in the middle of all this, surrounded by a lit candle featuring a grim reaper—*Santa Muerte*. There were also white and red candles all over the floor. The candles made the room extremely warm and smelled like a cathedral.

"What is all this?" said Sophie, studying every individual item in the living room. She picked up a sugar skull and admired its artistic designs—that's when she heard voices from the kitchen.

3

Sophie walked into the kitchen and was smacked with the delicious food smells—right at the source. When she looked at the dinner table, a flash of lightning lit the room, followed by a boom of thunder.

"Gr-Gruh-Grandpa?" said Sophie.

Sophie's Grandpa Thomas was scooting a chair out to sit in. The gray suit he was buried in was dirty with mud and filled with spots of moss on the shoulders. His head was bobbed down, his back was hunched, and his face was droopy. He was moving slowly. His bald head was covered in bits of moss and mud. His old man's cheeks were sagging—the same as when he was *alive*. He picked up his head slowly and gazed at Sophie with his milky white eyes that had light gray in the middle. His facial expression was blank. He raised an arm and waved at Sophie, side to side, without much effort. His fingers were bony and turning black.

Sophie's mom and dad looked at the kitchen entrance to see who Grandpa Thomas was waving at.

"Sophie!" said her dad, who was sitting down next to her mom. "I thought your mother and I told you to sleep!" He seemed angry and nervous.

Sophie's mom smiled at her husband and said, "No, No. It's okay, dear. Sophie missed her grandpa." Her eyes were full of tears.

Speechless and in shock, Sophie watched as her living-dead Grandpa Thomas took a seat at the table. Everything Sophie had smelled was perfectly placed on the table. Upon further inspection, Sophie also saw her Grandma Kayla sitting next to her husband, Grandpa Thomas.

Grandma Kayla looked horrible. She had one missing eye—a black void—and the lips and skin around her mouth were gone; crooked and missing teeth were fully exposed. She was wearing the red dress—now covered in moss—that she was buried in. The little bit of hair on her head was thin and white.

Sophie's heart was pounding—almost exploding. She felt she was going to faint. Was this real? Was this a dream? She couldn't tell anymore.

There was a knock at the door, three slow thumps.

"Well, since you're awake, can you go get the door, honey?" said Sophie's mom, full of cheer. "It must be your cousin Emily."

Emily had been dead for a year. She was killed in a horrendous car accident at only seventeen years old. She had to have a closed casket viewing because the crash wrecked her body and face.

The knocking continued.

Knock.

Knock.

Knock.

Lightning flashed.

Sophie turned to the living room, looked at the window, and saw a disfigured girl standing outside. She was wet from the rain. Her face was a mangled and twisted horror show of what it was before. It was as if her eyes grew apart from the last time Sophie had seen her—alive.

Sophie stepped back and fainted, falling headfirst on the kitchen floor.

MY BROTHER DANIEL

1

It was Thanksgiving morning. I drove into Devil's Hill, Arizona, to visit my parents. I was also going to see my strange brother Daniel. I was twenty-five years old back then, so Daniel was thirty-five years old at the time. In his mid-thirties, he was a man who still lived at home with his folks and never left home or intended to.

Daniel never had a girlfriend—or boyfriend. Come to think of it, I never knew which sex he preferred or if he even *wanted* to be in any kind of relationship with another person.

Our parents only had two kids. And I was the only one bringing in relationship-worthy females to meet them. But there was a string of ladies I kept away from mom.

But maybe it was Daniel's weight that kept him single? Daniel was about four hundred pounds and at least six feet tall. All he wore were tight overalls that he had had since he was a teenager.

He wasn't much to look at either. He was bald and looked like my mother's mom, my Gramma Jane, who wasn't much of a looker at all. The old lady used to give me the *creeps*. My mom had a disagreement with her a while back, so we didn't talk to her anymore—and for that, I'm glad, but I did get to see her in Daniel's face every time I saw him. Thank goodness he never smiled because if that were to happen, I'd see nasty old Gramma Jane ready to smother me with one of her wet kisses and warm hugs. Minus the old-lady Avon perfume she heavily coated on—it makes me shiver just thinking about it.

I was driving to my parents' home alone that morning because my wife, Elsa, didn't want to be around my brother anymore. She told me that he stared at her the whole time she sat across the table from him at the previous Thanksgiving dinner. Every bite of turkey he took, every mouthful of mashed potatoes he gobbled; he was staring at her. I guess I hadn't noticed because my dad was known to talk your ears off, and that was what he was doing to me. I believe he was talking about a mess his next-door neighbor got into while building a shed. And he was also making too much noise, and it was hard to get any sleep. But as Daniel sucked in a helping of canned cranberries and licked his fingers after greasing them with the butter dripping off his biscuit, he kept staring at Elsa. I asked her why she didn't look away from him or nudge me—tell me anything at all, and she said she felt scared and couldn't move. She told me she felt like a deer caught in the headlights of a big semi. And, of course, after my dad quit yapping my head off about his neighbor, I looked at Daniel, and he had his face aimed at his gigantic plate of Thanksgiving heaven. But I remember that Elsa gave me a weary smile—forced—

Christmas in the Empty Cabin

and asked me how the macaroni salad she had made was. After hearing that, I would say that Daniel is *indeed* fond of the ladies, but I can't be too sure. Not even now.

I guess Daniel had always been some sort of a creep. He was a sociopath. The guy had no feelings whatsoever, and his face never showed a sign of emotion. He could have sat down, watched a comedy film, and never laughed. You had a better chance of finding Big Foot than finding a smile on Daniel's face.

I also remember that he stayed in his room a lot. He would only come out to use the bathroom or get food or drink from the kitchen. I would never hear a good morning, hello, or goodnight from the guy.

It's funny how things start blooming in your mind once you start going down memory lane. All these small houses packed with forgotten memories start opening up to you, inviting you. One that opened up to me was remembering how Daniel murdered at least a dozen cats and dogs. He once had a pet turtle, but he killed it by cracking its shell with a rock down by the creek and severing its limbs. What's even more disturbing is that he murdered these innocent animals when he was a fully functioning adult in his mid-twenties.

I remember coming over to visit my parents one summer day when I saw him in the backyard axing a dog's body in half on the wood stump my dad used to cut wood on. After the top part of the dog's body fell off the wood stump, entrails right behind it, he continued to bash its brains in until the head was nothing but mush. I stood there until he was done. I just couldn't move; I probably didn't even blink. I was paralyzed with fear. When I could finally move, I returned to my car and drove home quietly. I told my parents about what had happened over the phone when I got home, but I never told Elsa—I didn't want to freak her out. My parents just shrugged it off and said that the dog bit Daniel or something that would never justify his actions to anyone but them. But maybe they were scared?

If he had any mental complications, my parents chose to ignore them and sweep them away like dust under a rug. But the elephant was definitely in the room, and that elephant would make its presence known that Thanksgiving morning.

2

I pulled up to the brown house at the end of Strawberry Avenue in the Grapevine neighborhood. The whole scenery looked like the epitome of autumn. If you could feel the cold, crisp air, it would have been the *definition* of autumn. There were tons of yellow and brown leaves on the floor; the sky was cold and dark blue, and the world seemed filtered in fall—it was beautiful, but what awaited me inside the house was the total opposite. It was worse than coming home to find Daniel murdering a dog.

As soon as I opened the front door of my parents' home, the rich smells of a Thanksgiving feast hit me: Turkey, gravy, stuffing, and pumpkin pie. These foods overpowered whatever else was ready to feast on, but I knew they were there for sure. What also hit me was the cold air inside the home. My parents were the type who cranked up the heater if it was seventy degrees—this was odd for sure. I was expecting the sudden heat

Christmas in the Empty Cabin

shock from stepping into an inferno, but all I received was a polar vortex.

I still had my hand on the doorknob as I stepped outside to check if my parents were home.

Yup.

My parents' car was still parked their car in the carport as I'd seen it, but I had to make sure.

I stepped back in and closed the door behind me. I said, "Mom? Dad? I'm here." I heard no reply. "Hello?" But I still heard nothing.

The kitchen light was on, and I noticed that it was the only light illuminated in the home. The curtains were still closed, and it looked like nobody had woken up that morning. When I stepped into the kitchen, I saw Daniel getting dinner ready.

"Hey! Brandon! Have a seat, bro. Here," he said as he pulled out a seat for me that already had a giant glass plate in front of it with the eating utensils on the side. "Would you like some wine? Beer? A Diet Coke or some Twist Mist Cranberry?"

I still remember how odd he looked. He was dressed in his same uniform of tight, dirty overalls, but the look on his face was different—it was disturbing. His eyes bulged out of his head, and he was sweating profusely. The smile on his face was genuine, but felt menacing. But even more disturbing was that he was talking—saying something! Daniel rarely even told me hi, so hearing him talking and interacting with me was weird.

I couldn't help myself, so I said, "Hey, what's gotten into you, buddy? You seem rather talkative today."

Daniel opened the oven, bent down, and took out the turkey. He closed the oven door with his grimy boot and said, "Well, I noticed how awful I was last

Thanksgiving—all my life, to be exact, so I thought I'd make it different this year. I want to talk more. I don't want to hide anymore, you know?"

I remember I smiled after he said that. I thought that Daniel was going to start acting normal. I would have an average functioning brother, but that was far from the truth; now I know it.

"Daniel, did you make the Thanksgiving dinner by yourself?"

"Yeah! I made the mashed potatoes from scratch! And no canned cranberries this year or store-bought pies. Everything is homemade, Brandon."

He sounded like a kid showing off a Lego Star Wars set he had completed.

"Sounds good to me," I said. "So, where are mom and dad? I'm pretty sure that this kitchen is the only room in this house that has any heat. And you know how annoying they get when it's cold. I'm glad it's chilly in here, though."

"I also made a fruit salad—it's extra good."

He had ignored my question. I took a sip of the soda he had served me and said, "Awesome. Daniel, where's mom and dad?"

Daniel put the corn and green beans on the table and said, "Why don't you go get them? I'm sure they're upstairs."

Oh, how I wish I never went up to go get them.

3

I got up from the table and started to the stairs. It was much colder in the other parts of the home. I walked up the creaky stairs and called for them.

"Mom, where are you? Dad, are you up yet?" But there was still no response.

As I stood in front of their bedroom door, something told me not to open it. I felt the sudden need to run away and just get out. Daniel was acting weird, and my parents not being awake was strange. Plus, the heater wasn't on.

I swallowed my fear and put my hand on the door. I called my parents one more time before going in, but I got no response. I opened the door slowly, and the smell of pennies drifted to my nose.

Two body shapes lay on the bed, covered by a white bedsheet that had blossoms of dark blood where the heads should be. I still remember the fright and anxiety that went all through my body. I didn't know if I wanted to cry, scream, or run. The only thing I did was start walking to the bed. I had to lift off the sheet. I had to see if they were okay or... dead. I couldn't dare see my parents dead—possibly *murdered*—but I had to see it with my own eyes.

I lifted the bedsheet, and the image was one I could not, and will never, get out of my mind. My parents had black, empty holes where their eyes should have been. Dry blood ran down from the sockets, creating dark red lines down their cheeks. Their mouths were also covered with blood—I didn't want to know why. I covered their faces again with the sheet and vomited all over the floor. Loads of puke splashed inside my dad's slippers. I felt terrible for doing that.

After getting rid of that morning's breakfast, I went to the door and called for Daniel.

"Daniel! It's mom and dad—they're... they're dead!"

My shout was followed by a minute of silence. Finally, Daniel replied, "I know. Come down here."

"You—you *know?* Daniel, did you... *kill them?*"

At that moment, I realized Daniel had upgraded from dogs and cats to mom and dad.

I knew this day would come. I saw it coming the very day I saw him with the ax.

"You're going to jail, Daniel! I can't *believe* what you've done!" I shouted as I made my way downstairs. I felt sick. I remember holding on to the walls as I made my way down. I was lightheaded, but also pumped with adrenaline. I was struck with grief and anger. I was mad at him for committing such an evil act and letting me have to see that.

Before I made my way into the kitchen, I was caught with a sudden shock of fear and realization: what if he was going to kill me next? I had no weapons—nothing. I grabbed the fireplace poker before going in, noticing it was caked with blood at the tip—my parents' blood. It had to be.

"Brandon, just come in here and enjoy dinner."

He wanted me to *eat* after I had seen such a horrible thing. Daniel snapped. I raised the fire poker in a baseball batting stance and walked into the kitchen.

My brother was sitting at the head of the table with a mountain of food on his plate. He looked like he always did: quiet, ugly, fat, and unfriendly. The chatty, smiling person I had seen when I had first walked in was gone.

"Sit down. Eat," Daniel said. His eyes were locked on mine. I felt intimidated.

"Daniel, you just killed our parents. Are you *serious?*"

"Weren't you tired of how they always looked at us? Tired of how it was always their way or the highway? Judging how we live, how we work, what we believe in?"

I looked at him dumbfounded and said, "Daniel, actually, they never gave you *anything* about that. I was the one who always had to deal with all of that. Those are the cons that *I* dealt with all of *my* life."

"Just sit down and eat."

"I'm calling the cops," I told him. Before I went to grab my phone, I noticed something horrific stuffed inside the turkey.

4

I couldn't believe what was lying inside the bird. Four eyeballs and two tongues served as the toppings of the brown stuffing that Daniel had cooked. Now I knew why my parents were eyeless and had bleeding mouths.

I had dropped the poker to the floor and pulled up a seat from the table to sit down before I collapsed from weakness. I took another look inside the turkey and looked away.

"Daniel," I said. "What in the *hell* did you do?"

He took a spoonful of mashed potatoes with a heavy coating of gravy and stuffed it in his mouth. I had always hated the way he held his spoon in a fist.

Daniel giggled. "You know... I don't know why I put their eyes and tongues inside the turkey. Maybe I did it because they were always watching and talking down on us. I thought it was a great gag, though—reminds me of something a B-Horror movie would feature, you know? Something like, 'Feast your eyes on this' or 'Jaw-dropping,' I don't know. Something like that." He laughed like a hyena.

I held my head in both hands and said, "This isn't a movie! This isn't normal!"

"Quiet down, Brandon," he said to me with an annoyed look. "Elsa will be here any moment now."

At that point, I had thought, Oh no… was he planning to murder Elsa and me? Were we going to become a "gag" for his b-rated horror scene?

I looked at him in disbelief and said, "You *what?*"

Daniel paid no mind to me. He started eating fruit salad, getting it all over his face. He put down his spoon and finally spoke up. "I thought you would be happy, Brandon. They always gave you crap. Last year after dinner, you all argued, remember? They were getting on your case and telling you that Elsa never lets you do anything? Saying how she's the *man* in the relationship, and she doesn't let you visit anymore? I swear dad said she has your balls in her purse."

I remembered that argument like it happened yesterday. My parents weren't fond of Elsa. Why? I believe it was because she didn't let herself. For instance, if someone—my mother—had something mean or rude to say, Elsa didn't hold back. I liked that about her.

"Daniel, I understand that you've always tried to look out for me, even if you never talked as much as you have today, but you killed—*killed* our parents! That's a lifetime in prison. In this case, the crazy house! Do you realize—*truly* realize what you've done?"

Daniel stopped eating and threw his spoon to the table. It bounced up in the air and landed by the turkey. I took a look at where it landed and felt sick. One of the eyeballs was looking at me with an eternal stare. Was it my mom's or my dad's? I didn't know and didn't care ever to find out. It's painful to remember such horror, but my therapist, Dr. Crane, tells me it's best to let everything out. Even if the scabs I'm picking at begin to hurt and bleed again. And in this case, the scabs I was reopening were everything that went on in the house that Thanksgiving Day.

After tossing the spoon, Daniel looked at me with crazy, angry eyes and said, "You've always been unappreciative, Brandon. You never thanked me for *anything*. That dog bit *you,* and *I* killed it. *I* killed it! You were too chicken shit to do anything about it. Years later, you're too chicken shit to face mom and dad and stand up to them, so I had to take care of it for you!"

The dog never bit me. I didn't know what the hell he was talking about. Daniel was going crazy.

"Daniel, calm down, okay? You need help. You need help more than ever, and I will ensure you get the best help you can get, okay?"

Suddenly, I heard a car pull up to the carport. It was Elsa. My heart started to race even more. I looked out the window from the kitchen and saw her getting out of the car.

Daniel looked out the window, and he got up from his chair. I picked up the poker from the floor and also stood up.

"Don't you dare touch her! Don't you dare, Daniel!"

He never stopped walking and never gave me a look. He said, "I'll be right back—I'm not going to hurt Elsa, and you shouldn't either."

"Why would I hurt her?" I asked him, confused.

I didn't know why he said that, and I still don't know why. Daniel went out the back door into the backyard. Was he getting a chainsaw? I didn't know. All I was thinking was I had to leave fast and take Elsa with me.

Before I could get to her, Elsa walked in and said, "Brandon, what's going on?"

She looked beautiful, even with concern on her face. Her blonde hair lay flat on her shoulders, and she wore a brown jacket. Her blue eyes were tense, and she looked serious, wanting answers. Before I could answer her, she said, "I know you called me about two hours ago. I barely saw the missed call until half an hour ago. I'm sorry, love. So, what happened?"

"Elsa, I never called you," I told her.

She looked at me with a frown. She opened her mouth and said, "Yes, you did. You—"

The poker was still clutched in my hand.

She took a look at it and said, "Why are you holding that?"

"It's Daniel... he killed our parents."

Elsa gasped and took a step back. I started to walk toward her, but then she said, "Stay away from me, Brandon. You stay the hell away from me. Get back!"

I stopped walking toward her and felt incredibly strange. Then a jolt of fear rushed at me because I knew she thought I had murdered them. I walked back to the table and placed the poker by the turkey. As soon as I did that, I heard her scream a high shrill of terror. She had seen the eyeballs in the turkey.

"What is *wrong* with you?"

"I didn't do this, Elsa! Why do you think I did this?"

"I should have known," she said as she walked back to the door. "I should have known."

Christmas in the Empty Cabin

"Should have known what?" I called after her. She opened the door and went running to the car. She slammed the front door in my face.

After struggling to open the warped, old wooden door, she was in her car and driving away. The tires screeched as she rode out of the neighborhood.

I didn't know what to do. I ran to the backyard and looked around—Daniel wasn't anywhere to be found. I was glad. Suddenly, my phone started ringing—it was Elsa.

"Elsa, why do you think it was me? How could I do something like that? It was Daniel who did it!"

"Brandon," she started. It sounded like she was crying and going hysterical. "Listen to me. Daniel is *dead*. He's been dead since before you... you... killed all those animals."

"Elsa, I never killed any animals! It was Daniel who killed them!"

She ignored my protests and said, "No. It was you. You have these small phases in which you think your brother Daniel is still around. When you're scared of facing situations that you don't know how to handle, you tend to do that. You're so messed up now that you don't even know what's real or not."

It was much colder outside, so I went inside to sit down. I couldn't believe what Elsa was telling me. Why was she saying this to me? I cleared my throat and said, "Elsa, I don't know what you're trying to do or who put you up to this, but you have no idea what you're talking about." I had to laugh at the whole situation.

"Brandon, I can't do this anymore. I love you—I love you *so much*, but I can't anymore. You're dangerous. The cops will be there anytime now. Goodbye."

Before I could say anything to her, the door busted open, and two cops came in and arrested me.

5

Long story short, I'm here at Woodland Asylum now on the east side of Devil's Hill.

I never saw Elsa again, and I miss her so much. I tried writing to her and calling her, but she never returned my letters or answered my calls.

Dr. Crane (you're the one reading this—yeah, you) told me to write everything down, and that's what I'm doing. That's how I remember it, and that's the truth. Dr. Crane says Daniel is dead—he even brought in a death certificate and a picture of his gravestone to prove it. But I think this is all some giant conspiracy shit against me. It was all a setup.

Elsa probably ran off with my boss and had me emitted. My parents were dead, and I was the perfect blame since I was there. Dr. Crane told me that Elsa said I went early to my parents' home, around five in the morning, because I would cook Thanksgiving dinner.

He told me why Elsa spent Thanksgiving with her parents. She said it was because I was giving her strange looks at the dinner table last year, and my parents and I had an argument. The argument happened, but I never looked at her that way—Daniel did. But I can't blame Elsa. It was all Daniel's fault.

The doctor says that I use Daniel as an alter ego or personality, but he's full of shit (sorry, Doc, you told me to write it all down). He tried telling me that I had resentment toward my parents for ignoring me when

Daniel died, but Daniel never died. I saw him kill that dog. I saw him.

My parents are dead, I lost my wife, and now I'm sitting here with many freaks and crazies as if I belong here—I don't. I just want to go back home.

I am looking forward to one thing, though. Daniel is coming to visit me tomorrow for Thanksgiving. Dr. Crane will finally meet him in the flesh.

THE HOUSE BY THE WOODS

1

Luke was obsessed with the house. After being released from Apollo Middle School, he stared at the structure with wonder each afternoon. He had never seen anybody inside the yard or even looking out the window. Whoever lived in the house was a mystery to Luke.

Luke lived in an apartment, so it could have been likely that he was obsessed with the home because it was a house. It was something he had always wanted since he and his mother moved out of his childhood home four years prior, but Luke felt there was more to it than that. There was something else about this particular home.

The house wasn't much of a looker—it was normal. The house was made of brick—the red blocks were left unpainted, and it had two windows in the front, like the eyes of the house. It had a wrought iron door in front of what had to be a wooden door. The house's roof was made for the snow, so it peaked in the middle. In Luke's hometown of Tucson, Arizona, the tops were all straight because it was in the desert. Snow caving in a roof was very unlikely.

The house was long, and Luke imagined what could be inside. He pictured a weird, ugly green rug like his grandmother had. He saw old pictures on the wall of people long dead. Embarrassing photos of someone as a naked baby, trinkets, and porcelain collectibles only old ladies fancied. A television that desperately needed an update, the aroma of nasty-smelling perfume, and the smell of grease and french fries from cooking home meals every day.

There was a small beige truck parked in the carport, but he never saw anybody driving it. It was old—it had to be from the '80s. Luke imagined that the driver was some tiny old man that went fishing regularly.

The back of the home was also wondrous to Luke. The backyard was surrounded by woods. Luke would have loved living in a house that had a giant wilderness waiting for him to adventure in. He imagined playing for hours. He saw the sun setting behind the bony arms and hands of the woods as his mother called for him to come inside because dinner was ready. Such lovely thoughts this house gave him.

Every day, Luke passed by the home and loved doing so. There were other homes next to it; it was the tenth home on the block out of fifteen, but this particular home just held Luke's attention.

Luke fell in love with the home in August, but it wasn't until November that he finally saw someone in the front yard.

When Luke was past the house, a curtain opened on the left side of the home. Somebody was watching him as they always did each time he passed by.

2

Being an 8th grader was tough for Luke. He was having a horrible time with math. He knew that he would have to work harder to make it to high school. He didn't want to be left behind in the 8th grade. So, on his way home, he had these thoughts of math and high school on his mind, so he was surprised when he saw a beautiful girl looking at him from the house he was always staring at.

Luke was so surprised to see someone standing in the yard that he stopped walking for a second. He cleared his throat, adjusted the backpack over his shoulder, and began to walk.

The girl was beautiful. She had to be about Luke's age. Luke studied her face and realized that he had never seen her before. Apollo Middle School was only two blocks from the house, so this girl had to be a student there, but Luke would have recognized such a beautiful face if he'd seen one.

Her hair was reddish-gold. It was wavy and hung by her freckled shoulders. She wore a pink tank top with Ren & Stimpy, jean shorts, pink ankle socks, and black Converse. It wasn't December yet, but the air was cold enough to make anyone wear jeans and a button-up. Hell, even a jacket. But the girl seemed unfazed by the autumn air.

She was standing on the left side of the home, leaning on the wall. She had a smile on her face. It was a smile so beautiful and so warm. Her pale skin was glowing in the early autumn sunshine. Everything about her was welcoming and comforting.

Luke kept walking, but it seemed as if he was floating. He was walking so slow and timid that, for a moment, he had forgotten where he was.

He wasn't one to regularly make eye contact with people. He usually kept his head down when walking in the halls or talking to other people, but that wasn't the case here. He locked eyes with the beautiful girl leaning against the wall with her shoulder. Luke felt himself smiling.

"Hey, I'm Erica. What's your name?" said the girl. She had a soft and friendly voice.

Luke stopped in his tracks. He turned around, ensuring she wasn't talking to someone else, and then proceeded to the front yard's chain-link fence. Luke walked up and placed his hands on the metal bar. "Um, hello, I'm Luke."

"Luke," said Erica, getting a taste of the name. "I like it. Well, hey, Luke, would you mind helping me find something?"

Luke's heart started racing. It wasn't every day that a pretty girl talked to him. He swallowed, and then he said, "Sure. I don't really have anything going on, anyway. Lose a cat or something?"

Erica laughed. "No, nothing like that. I was looking for something that I had lost in the woods. I had seen you walking by a few times, but I always felt a little iffy about asking for your help. It's because… ah, it's so embarrassing." Erica's freckled cheeks turned bright red. Her smile dropped as she looked at the ground, poking at some grass with the tip of her shoe.

"It's okay. You can tell me. I'm not some douche that will make fun of you or something." Luke thought about Greg Anderson at school. Now *that* was a douche.

Christmas in the Empty Cabin

Erica looked up and smiled. "Well, it's because I'm scared of the woods. I always feel a bear or ginormous spider will get me. And I'm always worried that I'll stay lost and forgotten forever. And what I'm looking for may just be under a log or a huge rock—I don't remember. So I also need help to get that out."

Luke nodded. "Sure! I'll be glad to help."

"Awesome! Let me open the gate for you." Erica walked over to the fence, and Luke noticed that she kept looking prettier and prettier the closer she got to him. He was usually in a trance with the house, but today he was mesmerized by its tenant.

Luke stepped inside the front yard of the home he had admired since he started 8th grade. He then remembered that he needed to call his mom. She would go ballistic if he didn't show up at his regular time.

"Hey Erica, do you mind if I use your phone? I should let my mom know that I'll be home later today. Otherwise, she will flip." Luke laughed and studied the house, trying not to drool over Erica's looks.

Erica's face took a different tone. It was as if she was suddenly terrified. She looked over at the house over her shoulder and said, "Um... yeah. My grandma isn't here right now. But we have to make it quick. I, uh, I don't really know how she would feel about some random boy being inside of her house with me. No offense, Luke."

"None took. I'll make it quick. I just want to let my mom know."

"Okay, let's head in." Erica walked to the door, not smiling again.

Luke started to think that maybe she was abused by her grandma, which was likely why he had never seen her outside or anything. He looked to the carport and saw that the little beige truck was gone.

3

When Luke walked inside the house, he realized it was nothing like he had imagined. The walls weren't white like his grandmother's; they were plastered with faux wood panels that reminded him of the walls inside his Uncle Jerry's trailer. There were also two small deer heads mounted on the wall.

The T.V. was the only thing like his grandmother's. And the home didn't smell of grease or fried potatoes; it smelled like a dirty hotel room with the lingering stench of cigarettes. A smell that was also dominant in his Uncle Jerry's trailer.

"The phone is over here. In the kitchen," said Erica. She stood between the living room and the kitchen. Her Converse was on the brown carpet—not green.

Luke picked up the phone, about to dial, when the beige truck pulled into the carport.

"Crap! That's my grandma! She'll kill you, Luke! Hurry! Let's go out the backdoor!"

Luke felt his heart pound against his chest like it wanted out. He immediately began to sweat. His pulse was pounding on the right side of his neck. He slammed the phone into the receiver on the wall and proceeded to the backyard with Erica.

Erica opened the back door and grabbed Luke's sweaty hand. "Let's go to the woods!"

They stepped out into the backyard, and he felt the sun wash over the coldness that the fright had given him. He and Erica stepped over the clean-cut grass, almost falling in it. They hopped over the chain-link fence and went into the woods.

After running into the woods, about twelve feet in, Erica stopped and motioned for Luke to do the same thing. "It's okay now. Whew! That was close." She had her hands on her knees, trying to catch her breath. Luke was doing the same thing, but he was scared as hell. It was something he would not admit to the beautiful girl standing before him.

Luke stood up and wiped the sweat from his forehead. "It's okay if I don't call my mom. She'll be pissed at me, but she won't blow her lid off. The worse thing she'll probably do is not let me watch the X-Men cartoon on Saturday morning." Luke fake-laughed and kicked a pebble into the base of a tree.

Erica smiled at him—a gorgeous smile—and then she looked over to her grandma's house. The backdoor opened, and her grandma came out with a cigarette in her mouth. She was of average height, chubby, and had white, short-cropped hair and wrinkly peach-colored skin. She wore a gray shirt with a catfish logo on the front and a pair of cargo shorts above her knees. She was standing by the door, looking around the backyard like she was searching for something. Maybe she had seen them, Luke thought.

"Um, I think we better do this some other time. How about tomorrow?" Erica asked.

"Sure! I can be here as soon as I get out of school. Is that okay?"

Erica nodded. "Sure! Thank you, Luke. Sorry about all this." She laughed and looked down at her shoes.

"Ah, it's nothing. I'll be glad to help. So do you go to Apollo?"

Erica looked up at Luke and looked away to her grandma's house. "Apollo? No, um, I go somewhere else. Look, I gotta go. See you tomorrow, okay?" She smiled again, making Luke's knees buckle. "Bye." She stepped up to Luke and hugged him. Luke was shocked. The only girls who had ever hugged him were blood related. Erica pulled back and started running toward the house, out of the woods.

Luke smiled as she ran away. He adjusted his backpack and decided he better go home the long way, not let Erica's grandma see him.

4

As Luke lay awake that night, he smiled as he gazed at the glow-in-the-dark stickers of stars and planets on his ceiling. He couldn't stop thinking about Erica.

He wondered why she didn't go to the same school he went to.

He imagined seeing her in the halls and during lunchtime. He saw them walking side by side to class. He imagined himself staring at her in a daze while in class. Maybe it was better that she didn't go to the same school. Erica was like his secret treasure.

Luke went to bed that night, drunk off the thought of Erica, and slept a happy, dreamless sleep.

5

Christmas in the Empty Cabin

School was finally out. Luke couldn't concentrate in class. All he had his mind on was Erica; he wanted to see her already.

He couldn't read *The Monkey's Paw*, couldn't solve stupid algebra problems, and didn't care about playing dodgeball in P.E.

He didn't care about cumulus clouds, could have cared less about some Tea Party, and ate his lunch in a trance, not paying attention. He almost bit into his milk carton, mistaking it for his chicken burger.

When the final bell rang, Luke nearly tipped over his desk, ramming it into some snobby girl named Marcia. She glanced back at Luke and gave him a look of disgust. Luke uttered "sorry" under his breath, fixed the desk, and went on his way to Erica.

Having been bright and dominant that morning, the sun was now tucked behind big, gray clouds. The wind was picking up, causing the air to drop a few degrees cooler. Luke untied the purple flannel across his waist and put it on; buttoned it up to block the cold.

I hope it doesn't rain; he thought. He didn't want anything to ruin his chances with Erica.

When Luke finally approached the house he was always so captivated by, Erica was nowhere to be seen.

Oh, no. Ah, come on.

He ran his hand through his hair, feeling the break of sweat on his head. *Where are you, Erica?*

Erica's grandma's truck was gone, so maybe she had left with her. Or maybe Erica was in trouble—grounded. Luke remembered how she kept looking back at her grandma when they were in the woods. The old lady seemed strict. Luke didn't doubt that she most likely grounded her granddaughter for any little thing.

Just as Luke was about to lose all hope and start walking home miserably, a familiar face came from behind the house.

"Luke! Hey!" Erica's smile was beautiful. And even though the sky was crowded with rain-filled clouds, Erica's gold-red hair still shone. She looked as pretty as she did the day before. She wore the same clothes: a Ren & Stimpy shirt and a pair of shorts. Luke wasn't one to judge. Maybe she had money problems. He had seen many kids at school get picked on for shitty things, like having holes in their clothes or wearing the same outfit for more than three days. Kids were cruel.

Luke walked over, smiling, and let himself into the yard. After closing the gate, he turned around, still smiling, and said, "I thought you weren't home. I had figured you left with your grandma."

Erica giggled. "No. I would never go with her. Trust me. She likes to steal sodas from the grocery store. She yanks cans off the six-packs and walks around the store, drinking it like nothing. When she's feeling careless, she munches on turkey sandwiches from the deli! It is so embarrassing."

Luke couldn't help but laugh. "I'm sorry. She's your grandma, and I'm laughing at her expense."

Erica waved a hand. "Oh, it's fine. Don't worry." The smile on Erica's face was replaced with one that matched the weather, dark and gloomy. And in a low tone, she said, "She isn't such a great person, anyway." Erica's eyes were staring at something off in the distance. She was lost in her head with her evil thoughts about her grandma.

Luke shuffled around in the grass awkwardly. He adjusted his backpack and sniffled.

"Oh!" Erica broke out of her trance and smiled. "Let's go into the woods! Are you still game to help me, Luke?"

She remembered my name, he thought lamely.

"Of course! Wanna get going?"

"Yeah. We better go now. Before my grandma shows up."

"Okay, let's do this."

6

Erica and Luke stepped into the woods. It was like a horror movie waiting to happen. The thunder started rumbling, and light rain started to come down, squeezing between the woods.

"So, what is it that we're looking for, exactly?"

Erica was in front of Luke, stepping on boulders as they made their way in deeper. She tossed her hair back over her shoulder. "Well, it's kind of hard to explain. It's a… box! Yeah, it's a box. It has some important stuff of mine in it. But the thing is, I can't get it."

"Why not?" Luke was stepping on the boulders now, too. He had grown tired of getting pine needles on his socks and shoestrings.

"Well, it's because the box is under some rocks, and I can't get them. You look pretty strong. I thought you were the man for the job."

Luke smiled and chuckled.

Erica looked back at him and smiled. "Plus, I don't want to be here alone." Her smile dropped, and she turned forward again, concentrating on the rocks they were stepping on.

Finally, a small creek appeared. Luke gasped as he saw it. The water was murky green, and drops of rain were rippling the body of water. The rain was coming down much more steadily now. Thunder boomed.

Erica looked back and noticed the expression on Luke's face. "You've never seen this before?" Her hair was wet, clinging to her beautiful face.

"No! This is awesome! We should hang out here more often. Especially now for fall break!"

Erica took on a sullen look and gazed at the clouds above.

"So, are we getting pretty close to the box? I don't think we should be out in the rain. It's coming down harder. And I don't want to get hit by—"

Lightning flashed, followed by a clap of thunder.

Erica laughed. "Yeah, let's get going! The box should be over there. More into the woods." Erica pointed at an opening by the right side of the creek.

When they finally reached the woods again, Luke saw a pile of boulders next to a bare tree. "Is it there?"

Erica was on Luke's right side, but she leaped to the front when she saw the rock formation he had pointed to. She ran in front of it and said, "Yes! I think this is it! This has to be where I buried it!" She went to the rocks, checking them all out quickly.

"Okay. Go ahead and stand back. I'll start the job." Luke stepped forward, dropped his backpack, went to the rock pile, and removed the small boulder at the very top. The boulders weighed a ton, but the task was doable. The weightlifting in P.E. last week had actually paid off.

Erica sat on a tree stump away from the pile. She watched Luke with eagerness.

Thunder boomed again, and rain began to fall dramatically now. Luke didn't care. He wanted to help

Christmas in the Empty Cabin

Erica. He tossed every boulder he put his hands on to the left. His back and arms would be aching in the morning, but it was totally worth it for Erica. Raindrops pelted all over Luke. His hair was a shaggy mess, and his clothes were swimming pool wet.

A hand appeared when Luke removed the last rock before the bottom one on the ground.

Luke jumped back and fell on his ass. He felt the mud squish below him, ruining his jeans and some of his flannel.

"What is it, Luke?"

Luke turned to Erica, but he couldn't get the words out. He wanted to say that he saw a hand, but the words were stuck.

Luke licked his lips and got back up. He didn't want to scare Erica, nor did he want her to see if it was what he thought he'd seen. Luke walked over to the rocks and—yup. It was a hand.

"What is it, Luke? Are you okay?" Erica asked from the stump she was sitting on.

Luke returned a fake smile and put a thumbs up in the air. "Yeah! I just fell on my butt. Stupid rocks tripped me. I guess I have butter feet!"

Erica nodded and looked away.

Luke's smile dropped as he turned again and gazed at the hand. The hand was small, ghostly pale, and had cuts and minor bruises on the fingers. Someone was buried under the rocks. But if someone was going to put a body there, why the hell would they just dump it under a pile of small boulders? And right next to a creek where people most likely hang out and play at?

Luke reached out his index finger to the hand and went slowly. He imagined the worst. He saw himself about to touch the finger when suddenly the hand came alive and grabbed his wrist, revealing some undead ghoul hungry for flesh. But Luke had to be brave.

When Luke lightly touched the hand's index finger, he felt it was ice-cold. He shot his hand back as if the touch had stung.

Whoever it is, they're dead, he thought.

Luke had to take the rest of the rocks off. Maybe there was a body under there attached to the hand. He didn't know if he wanted a body to be there or not. A dead body or a severed arm will haunt his dreams for the rest of his life. He looked back at Erica. She was still looking off in the distance, letting the cold rain hit her. He started lifting more rocks.

Luke started removing the boulders piled where the arm should be, and sure enough, the arm was intact. The arm was pasty white and covered in dirt and bruises. Luke was scared but needed to help somehow; he felt it in his gut. He started to remove all the rocks feverishly.

"Did you find it?" Erica called, sounding worried, watching as Luke was tossing the rocks faster now.

Luke was panting. "Um... I think so. Hold on. Stay back, Erica. I don't want you to get hit by any of the rocks." Luke tossed some boulders over his shoulder to make a point. Erica nodded and looked at the creek, watching the rain land on the green water.

Luke was working the rocks where the chest should be. When he lifted the final boulder, he saw the shirt. Thunder shook the sky. The shirt was of Ren & Stimpy, just like Erica's. Luke looked back at Erica. She wasn't looking his way. Good. He started to remove the boulders from where the face was.

At that point, Luke didn't care what kind of horror awaited him beneath the rocks. He had already seen plenty of horror films without his mom's consent. He

Christmas in the Empty Cabin

would have to deal with it if he had to see some result of a gruesome murder. Someone was buried here—left alone and covered in rocks. Dead or alive, he needed to help. He couldn't let something like blood, or a disfigured face or head stop him from checking on the body below. There was somebody out there who was missing a child or a sibling.

The final rock on top of the face was now there. Luke looked at Erica, who was still distracted by the creek. He turned back and lifted the final rock. The face underneath gave him a horrible shock.

7

It was as if Luke suddenly went deaf. The sounds of the rain falling were muted. The thunder rumbling was gone. He didn't feel the sweat dripping down his face or the freezing rain. He just felt a heavy feeling in his stomach. His heart was racing as it had never done before.

The face below was Erica's face.

It was Erica's face, but the head was caved in on the right side. The girl had a nasty dent in her temple. Black blood was piled on the rocks that were near her head. And the gore was smeared on the right side of the girl's face. Her left eyelid was partially opened, revealing a gray iris.

"Oh my God," Luke uttered. He felt his knees go weak. All the courage he was mustering was deflated and gone.

"You found it."

Luke jumped up and turned around, startled by Erica's presence. He moved in front of her view to block the body.

"F-found what?"

"I knew she didn't bury deep—not yet, I guess."

"What are you talking about? I-I-I didn't find the- the box yet."

Erica's face looked tired. Her voice was monotone. Her hair was wet with rain, and so were her clothes. She stood in front of Luke as if everything was normal.

"There is no box, Luke. I needed somebody to find the body—*my* body. I can only move and touch so much. I tried lifting the boulders, but I couldn't. I figured I would just get some help. And someone to go to the police."

Realization truly hit Luke. He looked at the dead girl, and there was no doubt about it; it was Erica.

"Y-you're *dead?* How?"

Erica picked up her head and looked into Luke's eyes. Everything went white, and Luke saw what had happened to Erica.

8

Two months before, Erica and her grandma were in the backyard of their home. The day was sunny and bright. The last days of summer were clinging to the air. Erica was putting the lawnmower away in the small shed behind her grandma's home. Her grandma came up to her. She was holding a hammer, getting ready to fix the windowpanes.

"Now, you can start cleaning the dishes inside."

Christmas in the Empty Cabin

Erica turned around to face her. Her face was sweaty, and her hair was a mess. The Ren & Stimpy shirt she was wearing was clinging to her skin.

"I have to get some rest for school tomorrow, grandma. All I've been doing are chores."

Erica's grandma's face changed as if she had been smacked by some invisible hand. "I don't give a damn that you have to go to school tomorrow. You have to do your goddamn chores. You're living with *me* now. Your mom and dad are as dead as roadkill, and they ain't here to keep you. You think I want you here? You think I do? God, no! You're just a check to me now, little girl. Now get your ass inside and wash the damn dishes."

Erica's eyes watered up, threatening to drip tears down her dirt-smeared cheeks. She felt the sadness ball up in her throat. She felt the anger swell up in her fists as she tightened them. Her chest was about ready to explode with frustration. She was sick and tired of taking abuse from her grandma.

"You're... you're such an old and ugly *bitch,* and I wish *you* had died!" It was out. Erica couldn't take it anymore. Two months of physical and verbal abuse was just too much for her to take.

Erica's grandma was enraged. She had never been spoken to this way in all of her life. And the little shit in front of her had never spoken back before. She raised the hammer she had in her hand and connected it to the side of Erica's right temple as hard as she could. The last thing Erica saw was a bright flash of light before blacking out forever. Erica's body collapsed on the grass. The wound on her temple was horrid.

Erica's grandma stepped back in shock. She didn't know she would hit the girl that damn hard. There was so much blood—it happened so fast. When she called her old and ugly, talking back, she just lost it. But now, what the hell was she going to do? She killed her granddaughter. Erica's skull was cracked and bleeding. The hammer did a gruesome job of caving the poor girl's temple in.

Grandma had to move fast. She put Erica's body in a wheelbarrow and proceeded to the woods.

The grandma was at the spot where Luke now stood. There were boulders everywhere, left from some landscape construction that never happened. She had brought the shovel along to dig a hole. She was about to start when she heard kids playing. She looked out to the creek and saw the kids skipping rocks.

"Shit!" She had no time to dig a hole. She didn't want to be seen. She took Erica's body off the wheelbarrow and placed her on the ground. Her temple was leaking blood and cranial fluid. She started piling the rocks on her body, covering what she had done. She had planned to go back and bury her deep, but she gave up on the idea. Let some wild animal pick the flesh off of that rotten little girl. Erica's grandma forgot about the whole thing.

When the truancy officer from Apollo Middle School asked about Erica's whereabouts, she told him she had run away.

9

"I guess she never came back to bury me. She was probably hoping an animal would smell me and eat my body," said Erica, looking at her corpse.

Luke was stunned. He was staring at Erica with his mouth open, eyebrows scrunched. "But... how can it be? How is this happening?"

Erica smiled. "I don't know, Luke. But thank you so much for helping me. I think I can rest now. I just couldn't go away until my body was found. She has to pay."

"But... how?" Luke just couldn't understand anything that was going on. A dead body? A ghost? A murder? It was all too much. He started to feel angry. "This isn't fair! It isn't fair, Erica!"

Erica's smile dropped, and now she was the one confused.

"It isn't fair. Are you going to go away now? Why? I like you, Erica. You were, like, the first girl I ever truly *like-liked.* And you were the only person who was nice to me in this stupid town! This isn't fair!" Luke's eyes watered up, and the tears started rolling off his cheeks.

Erica came forward and hugged him. She held him tight. Luke embraced her and started to sob. He didn't care if a girl saw him crying. This was all too much for him. He was feeling a whole spectrum of emotions, and he just couldn't deal. He started to feel bad about being selfish, wanting Erica here for him, and thinking about himself. Erica was dead. He was alive. He helped find her body, and that was important.

They stopped hugging and looked at each other. Erica spoke. "I'll miss you, Luke. You helped me move on. Thank you so much."

Luke smiled and wiped the tears from his eyes. The rain had stopped falling. He looked up, and Erica was gone. Luke looked all around for her; she was nowhere. He felt a chill breeze pass by his face. He grabbed his backpack off the ground and started to walk home.

10

Luke went home that night and told his mom about the body he had discovered by the creek. When they called the cops, Luke bent the truth and told the detectives he had seen the young girl and an older woman in the woods arguing. He also mentioned seeing the woman in the front of a house with a small beige truck parked out front. The cops knew where to go.

11

When fall break was over, Luke was walking home from school. The house he had always admired now stood empty. The truck was gone, and the windows were bare. The old lady was doing her time.

When Erica didn't come out, Luke smiled.

CHRISTMAS BLUES

Barry felt he had to do it, but he was scared to death about the deadline that would ensue. The man in the black suit told him to think about it for a minute or two, and either he walked away or made a deal. The sun had just fallen behind the woods' skeletal arms that touched the cold, crisp air. The sky was a cool purple and blue. Stars were beginning to shimmer enough to say hello. Dusk was here.

This place was miles away from Barry's home. He told his family he was going on a trip with his friend Mark to do some yard work for folks that lived in a mansion. He promised he would come back with money. He told his kids they'd get a Christmas tree and decorations for their home. It was a lie, but a small one. Well, not really. This lie would haunt him for the rest of his days if he decided to make the deal.

Barry closed his eyes outside a small local bar in a rural area and paced back and forth. Christmas music played loudly for the drunkards inside.

Christmas. Christmas, he thought.

His wife, Erica, needed clothes, Tommy needed clothes, and Beth also needed things.

It's the most wonderful time of the year.

For the rich and upper-middle-class, it is indeed a wonderful time. Christmas trees, expensive gifts tucked underneath, honey hams, booze, egg nog, cookies, and ugly sweaters, they can all afford to experience a wonderful time. Barry was far from that.

You're thirty years old. The man will want to see you in twenty years, but twenty isn't enough. You will miss out on your wife and your kids! Will they be okay? Of course, they will. He said they will. And if things go as they should, they'll be financially set.

Barry shook his head slowly and kept walking in front of the bar.

No one has called you for a job—it's been three months! And besides that, your paintings aren't selling, the rent will be due in three weeks, there are barely any groceries…

Barry opened his eyes. He looked toward the path in front of the bar that led to the crossroads where famous jazz musicians and desperate men had walked before him. He saw the man in the black suit appear in the middle.

It was time.

Barry walked to him.

"Merry Christmas," said Barry to himself.

CHRISTMAS IN THE EMPTY CABIN

1

Jake woke up shivering because of a coughing fit that had left his chest in pain. The harsh, cold temperatures had given him a bad cold. He now thought he might have pneumonia.

"Where the hell am I?" Jake said to himself.

He was lying on cold, hard ground. He opened his eyes and realized he was in a cave. The jagged rocks hung above him like a roomy casket.

Jake attempted a sigh, but only started coughing again. "I was hoping it was only a bad dream." He cleared his throat and rubbed his chest with a gloved hand.

The realization hit Jake like an icy, hard snowball. He had been camping out in the woods with his best friend since elementary, Daniel Goodman. Right before a freak blizzard settled in the night before, Daniel slipped and got his foot stuck between two boulders. Daniel fell over, causing his ankle to break, and the bone cut through the skin. The temperature had dropped significantly within minutes, so Daniel was bundled up with his and Jake's blankets and extra clothing. Daniel, unable to walk, stayed inside his tent as Jake went out to get help.

Jake scoffed and sat up, wincing. "Yeah. Some rescue effort, aren't I? Fell asleep in a goddamn cave."

As Jake sent out for rescue, the blizzard had become too much to bear. His eyeballs felt like they were about to freeze, obscuring his view even more. His whole body was numb, and the coughing had started. Feeling exhausted and unable to carry on, Jake found refuge in a cave. The cave was still utterly cold, but he needed some rest. He had walked over two miles in the fierce winds.

He looked towards the cave's opening and saw that not much had changed since he retreated inside. The ground was still a piercing white, the wind was howling ghostly, and snow was still falling from the sky in rapid flurries. But it was much calmer than when he had first set out for help.

Jake got up, wincing some more from the pain all over his body, and checked his phone to see if he could get any network signal. The last time he checked, it was still searching for one.

"Great. The stupid thing is dead now." Jake buried the phone in his pocket and walked towards the cave's opening. He looked out and saw snow-capped pine trees far in the distance. It had to be the same pine trees surrounding the back of the cabin he and Daniel had seen. They had both noted how odd it was for someone to live in recluse, stuck at home, in the middle of the Rockies. The cabin was miles away from civilization. It made Jake think about *The Shining*.

Jake unwrapped the scarf around his neck and put it over his mouth. He stepped out of the cave and into the freak blizzard that ruined his and Daniel's camping trip.

2

The sky was gray, meaning the time had to be around 5 p.m. It would be night soon. Jake had to hurry and power through the snow if he wanted to rescue himself and Daniel. His tread in the snow had gotten much slower. His boots were plunging right into the ice, about a foot at least. The icy flurries struck the exposed part of his face relentlessly. His whole body was numb, but that small space between his nose and eyebrows started to sting.

Jake heard wolves howling in the distance.

"Ah, great! Just what I needed!" Jake started laughing. All he and Daniel were going to do was have an annual December camping trip. A trip that they both started in High School, back in 2006. Suddenly, there was a massive field of clouds in the sky. Winds picked up, snow started falling, and Daniel broke his ankle. Jake shook his head and started laughing some more. The maniacal laughter cut off abruptly when Jake began coughing again. The fit lasted much longer than it had in the cave.

Oh, have mercy on me. Please! Don't let it be pneumonia. I want to see Sheryl and Phillip.

Sheryl was Jake's wife of eleven years. They married fresh out of high school a year later. Phillip was their ten-year-old son. Even though Daniel was freezing and hurt and in dire need of rescue and medical help, his family was the real motivation for keeping him on his feet.

The cabin was now only a few yards away. Jake was feeling sleepy and beyond exhausted. His body was so cold that he started to feel too hot for his garments. He wanted to strip off his clothing and cool off in the wind, but that wasn't logical.

"No, it isn't. But I'm *hot*. How the hell am I hot? I don't know. Like how the hell did this blizzard happen? I. Don't. Know!" Jake screamed through the snow flurries. His walking started to feel like he was pushing inside a swimming pool. His effort started to strain the muscles in his calves and thighs. It was a far more strenuous hike than he had perceived.

Daniel could die. He could be dead. God, no. Please let me get there quickly. Think about Sheryl; think about Phillip. Come on, Jake, come on!

Jake looked up from the snow-covered ground and saw a black figure standing on the left side of the cabin. They must have seen that Jake noticed them because they started to wave at him. Jake raised a hand in the air, unintentionally giving the peace sign.

Ah, thank God.

The flurries were now making it too hard to see. Ice kept getting in Jake's eyes.

The wolves started howling again. From the sounds, it sounded like a pack of four or five, hungry for fresh meat. The wolves were close now. If Jake had turned around, he would have seen five of them ready to pounce on him.

I have to hurry. Think about Daniel, think about Sheryl, think about Phillip. ThinkaboutDaniel—thinkaboutSheryl—thinkaboutPhillip.

Jake, feeling colder than he had earlier—no longer feeling hot, started trudging through the snow with

Christmas in the Empty Cabin

some newfound speed. When he looked at the cabin, the figure was gone. They must have gone inside.

The wolves started howling again. Jake could hear them on the snow now.

The cabin was now only a few feet away. It stood in the middle of nowhere; only pine trees surrounded the backyard. It was a mahogany cabin that had two stories. No smoke was coming out of the chimney.

Jake paid no mind to those small details. He had a pack of wolves hunting him down and the cold bite of a blizzard at his chest. He started wondering which was going to kill him first.

Before Jake knew it, he was right in front of the steps that led into the cabin. Jake smiled and climbed the steps, gritting his teeth as his legs wobbled without strength. The wolves started running behind him.

Jake fell against the door and turned the knob. It was locked.

Jake removed the scarf from his mouth and started hollering and banging on the door. "Hello? Let me in! *Please!* There are wolves out here!"

Jake turned around and saw the wolves gathered at the bottom of the steps. Like obedient dogs, they sat and waited for their meal to get closer. Jake let out a small moan. He turned back around and started his ruckus some more.

"Please! Let me in! *Please!* The wolves! I need—"

The sound of the door unlocking made Jake stop in mid-sentence.

3

Jake opened the door and pushed himself in. Before shutting the heavy wood door, he caught a glimpse of the wolves. They were still sitting by the steps as if they were awaiting a snack or for someone to come out and retrieve them. Jake shut the door and let out a sigh of relief.

Jake had one hand on the cold wood of the door, the other hand on his rattling chest. "Thank you... so much. I appreciate you—"

When Jake turned, there was nobody there. The house was dark and empty. The living room was bare except for a badly worn couch, an oak coffee table, and a lake painting surrounded by woods. The painting hung crooked. The windows, thankfully, were not broken or damaged.

Right in front of Jake were the stairs that led to the second floor. Jake glanced up there and saw that two doors were closed, and one was open.

"Hello? Anybody here? I saw you outside... waving at me. Hello?"

Nobody answered back. Jake frowned.

It was cold inside the cabin, but it wasn't nearly as cold as outside. There was no bitter wind or snow to be felt.

Jake wiped his boots on a very old welcome mat, leaving behind water and ice, and decided to start for the kitchen on the right of the stairs. Like the living room, the kitchen was bare except for a few items and furniture. Luckily, a semi-used candle and a box of wooden matches were on an old wooden table. Jake quickly went for them and struck a match, igniting the

Christmas in the Empty Cabin

candlewick. Jake removed his wet gloves and put his hands close to the small flame.

"Ah. *Good God.* This will do."

It was great to feel warmth again. Good warmth. Not the warmth that Jake was feeling due to being so cold.

Jake looked around the kitchen as he warmed his hands up. He would check the old Frigidaire fridge first. He looked outside and saw the wolves running away together to the pines.

"Yeah. Shoo, you little bastards."

Jake bit his tongue when he thought about Daniel. *What if the wolves go to him?*

They won't.

Jake shook his head and walked over to the fridge. When he opened it, he saw a bottle of water, a wedge of cheddar cheese, and an apple that had already gone bad.

Jake rushed for the water and drank greedily. Once he stopped, his chest started to hurt again, causing a violent coughing fit.

After Jake was done coughing in pain, he composed himself and walked over to the stairs. He went back into the kitchen to retrieve the candle. He took the top cardboard piece off the box of matches, put a hole in the middle, and used it as a wax catcher as he held the candle.

"Hello? I'm coming up. I have no weapons, and I'm not here for anything bad. I need a phone. My friend, Daniel, is still out there in the blizzard. He broke his ankle."

The sound of silence was all Jake got back. Then the howling wind and ice began pelting against the windows and the cabin.

"I'm coming up!"

Jake walked up the steps, creaking the old wood as he ascended. Since the other doors were closed, Jake went to the open one. Jake walked in and saw a bed neatly made with a white sheet, a fluffy pillow, and a nightstand with an oil lamp. There was only one window in the room. Jake went to it and saw that the snow was still coming down, with no signs of stopping. The wind seemed to have been picking up more speed.

"Dammit, Daniel. Please be okay. *Please.*" Jake started coughing again. When he started for the bedroom door, he felt a wave of nausea and dizziness. He touched his forehead and felt that it was blazing with heat.

It's pneumonia.

"Stop it! Now let's find a phone."

Jake walked down the stairs and searched for a landline; he didn't find one.

Jake decided to wait on the couch. Maybe the person who waved him down would be in soon.

As Jake looked out the window in the living room, watching an endless white winter, he started thinking about his wife.

"I should have listened to you, babe." He chuckled as he watched the snow swirl in the sky. "I really should have listened to you. I wouldn't even mind hearing you say 'I told you so' on repeat for the next year."

Before the trip, Sheryl had told Jake that she had a bad feeling about it. Jake reassured her that everything would be fine; it would only be two days. They had supplies if anything were to happen to them.

Sheryl still didn't like the idea. The whole thing did not sit right with her. It was the first time she had voiced concern about Jake and Daniel's camping trip

Christmas in the Empty Cabin

to the Rockies every December. Jake didn't know what to make of it, but he thought Sheryl was just being Sheryl: always nervous and stuck on thinking something terrible would happen.

Jake scoffed. "But something bad *did* happen. Great." He pressed his hot forehead against the stinging cold window. He sighed deeply. "I'm so sorry, Sheryl. I love you, babe. Always."

And what about Phillip? Phillip would be devastated if something wrong happened to his dad. He would—

Jake cut those horrible and awful thoughts about his boy and started looking for wood near the fireplace—there was none. Jake wanted to cry but didn't let himself. Even alone, cold, and lost, he was still too proud to shed a tear on his lonesome.

After two hours of waiting, Jake began to get sicker.

4

Burning with fever, Jake started to shiver violently. He removed his bubble jacket and used it as a blanket. He looked out the window from the couch and saw that it was now darker outside. The sky was a dark purple, layered with clouds. The snow had stopped falling, but the wind was still fierce.

Jake laid down and covered up with his jacket. The couch was a two-seater, so it was uncomfortable for a man of six-foot and two inches. Plus, his neck was starting to hurt from the armrest. But stricken with illness and exhaustion, Jake drifted to sleep within seconds.

5

Jake had fallen asleep and dreamt that he and Daniel were trapped inside his tent. Figures started to appear like shadows on the yellow tent. Wolves started biting and pawing the tent to pieces as he and Daniel screamed in terror. Once the tent was no longer standing, the wolves went for the two men. Two wolves went for Daniel's face and neck, tearing the flesh and drawing pints of warm blood. Jake could do nothing but scream in horror.

Once he started screaming, the wolves pounced on him and bit down hard. That was when he woke up.

"Ah! God! Oh, my goodness." Jake woke up on the couch and started coughing, hurting his chest. His fever had worsened, and his body was hot enough to melt snow.

Jake dizzily looked around and saw that it was night outside.

Dammit. How long have I been out?

Jake sat up a little, grimacing from the pain all over his body, and looked around the cabin. It was still only him inside the home. There was no sign of anybody; nobody had arrived.

The candle was almost to the end. Jake decided to go upstairs. Wherever the owner was, he didn't care anymore. He had to sleep his fever off, whether he was imposing or not. Being polite was the least of his worries now. He felt horrible about leaving Daniel out there, but at least he had left him with a small, portable heater. And in reality, if Jake tried to retread the snow, he'd die of pneumonia. If he wanted to save his best friend, he'd need to get rest first. And if nobody showed up, he would have to walk four miles into town.

I better get some sleep now.

Jake remembered the bed upstairs with a pillow and an actual sheet and decided to ditch the old couch. Swaying and walking ever so slowly, Jake grabbed the candle and went upstairs to sleep.

After Jake stripped down from his still mildly wet clothes, he got under a fluffy comforter and thanked God. The bed was soft. And in comparison to the ground in the cave, it was a goddamn *cloud.*

He finally felt the warmth he longed for. He was in a soft, comfortable cocoon of warmth. He was still burning with fever and dizzy from the sickness, but he bundled up anyway and drifted off to sleep.

6

Jake woke up three hours later. He would never know it, but it was midnight.

He had woken up because there was way too much noise from downstairs. He opened his eyes and looked toward the door; somebody had closed it.

The owner must be here.

Jake heard what sounded like a real live party. He heard laughter, bickering, shouts of excitement, and music—Christmas music. "Rockin' Around the Christmas Tree" by Brenda Lee was playing.

Jake got out of bed, only in his long Johns, and wrapped himself with the white sheet. He was still cold, but he no longer felt faint or dizzy. The wheezing and rattling sound in his chest was gone. He no longer felt pain from his hike or the fever.

Guess I just really needed some good rest.

Jake slipped on his boots and walked over to the bedroom door. He wrapped the blanket tighter around his back and turned the knob.

After he opened the door, Jake's eyes opened wide. He had the surprise of a lifetime.

7

As soon as Jake opened the door, warmth hit him in such an enticing and beautiful way. There was a yellow light all over the once-dark cabin. He saw shadows moving and swaying on the walls. The voice of Brenda Lee sang smoothly and merrily over the rock and roll music of her time.

Jake stepped out of the room, gripping the sheet over him like an old woman's shawl.

He looked down and couldn't believe his eyes.

About twenty people were gathered in the living room. Most of them were couples, dancing closely as the music played on an old record player. There was an enormous Christmas tree set by the window where Jake had been looking out earlier. The tree was very old-timey. It was adorned with silver tinsel, popcorn on a string, huge Christmas lights in assorted colors, and a giant star at the top. There were also presents wrapped in green and red shiny paper under the tree.

The fireplace was roaring. The fire was healthy and bright, breathing oxygen hungrily. There was a table filled with foods like honey-glazed ham, fruit cake, mashed potatoes, corn, biscuits, cookies, candy canes, and two bottles of wine.

The crowd in the living room paid no mind to Jake. He stayed frowning as he tried to digest what he was witnessing.

Some people looked as if they had crawled out of the '50s, some from the '80s. One person looked like a hipster. It all just didn't make sense.

One of the closed doors opened up on the left of Jake, and a couple came out. A young man resembled Buddy Holly—he even had the same black plastic frames. The guy came out smiling, zipping up his pants, and buttoning them up. Jake saw a girl behind him, fixing her skirt and patting her blonde hair. They both looked like they came from the '50s.

"Oh, gee. Sorry, mister. We didn't know anyone was up here. My apologies, sir," said the Buddy Holly look-a-like. He looked down in embarrassment and reached for his lover's hand. When the guy looked back at Jake, Jake noticed something strange: a small wound on the guy's forehead. Dried black blood ran down from the hole in his head to the bridge of his nose.

As the guy walked downstairs, Jake saw that his companion was beautiful. The only flaw the young woman had was a slit throat. Her blouse was a bloody mess. She looked at Jake shyly and kept her blue eyes on the floor. She followed the Buddy Holly-looking lad down the stairs. Jake saw that their fatal wounds weren't showing anymore; they were perfectly normal.

Jake was in shock. He stepped back, almost entering the room he had been sleeping in again.

"This fever is giving me one messed up dream. What in the hell is—"

"That's Teddy Bauer and Rachel Flanagan. They were only seventeen when they were murdered out here in the woods around Christmastime."

Jake spun around and saw a figure standing in the shadows of the room he was staying in.

"Gah! Who the hell are you?" Jake gripped the sheet tighter around his head.

The figure stepped out. It was a woman of about thirty years old. She was wearing a gray sweater, black jeans, and boots, and she had her brown hair in a bun. The yellow light from downstairs illuminated her face. She was beautiful and peaceful looking.

"Hello. I'm Claire. Claire Bennett. I was the one who waved you in. Outside?"

Jake sighed and put a hand to his heart. "My goodness. You really scared me!" He laughed and let himself loose. "Thank you so much for letting me in your place. I was almost eaten alive by wolves. The snow was almost killing me."

"You're safe now, okay?" Claire smiled warmly.

"Wait a minute." Jake paused and scrunched his eyebrows together. "Did you just say that the couple downstairs was *murdered?*"

"Teddy and Rachel? Yes. They were murdered by a serial killer in 1956, dubbed the Rocky Slasher. Those two were making love in their car when the psychopath showed up. He shot Teddy in the head and slit Rachel's throat."

Jake smiled. "You're kidding me, right?"

Claire shook her head slowly. "No. Not at all. As a matter of fact, everyone down there is dead. Suicides, murders, accidents, you'd be surprised. Every Christmas, we meet here and have a party. This is where all the lost souls come to once they discorporate from their bodies. They've been doing this for years. I barely showed up three years ago. And, of course, you have to be nearby."

Jake's heart started racing. "Wait. Are you saying you're *dead?*"

Claire walked closer to Jake and showed him her neck. She had a purple and black ring all around it. A bone was protruding, stretching out the skin on the left side of her neck.

"Oh, my God!" Jake stumbled backward and put a hand to his mouth.

"I'm sorry, Jake. I didn't mean to scare you. Look, why don't we just go downstairs, and I'll introduce you to everyone?"

"You're just the owner, right? Playing tricks on me? Where have you been? Why did you call me over, unlock the door, and disappear?"

"The Christmas Song" by Nat King Cole started playing on the record player downstairs. The crowd below still didn't bother with the commotion from Jake upstairs.

Claire looked down. "I'm sorry about that. I sensed another soul in the distance."

Jake looked up, startled. "Huh? Who?"

Claire pointed to someone below.

Jake looked to where she was pointing—it was Daniel.

8

Daniel walked into the living room from the kitchen. He was dressed as they came on the camping trip: a yellow bubble jacket, black jeans, boots, and a black beanie. He was holding a cup of coffee in both hands.

Jake ran down the stairs.

"Hey, Jake! It's good to see you again, buddy!" Daniel set his coffee down on the table with all the other food and drinks.

Jake ran up to him and embraced him tightly. "I'm so sorry, man. I didn't want to leave you. I fell asleep in a cave—then I fell asleep in here. I swear I was going to get help, man. I had just got really sick."

Daniel smiled. "Hey, there is no need to explain yourself. I know what happened. Claire filled me in. Let me tell you, I feel much better now. Before I... died from hypothermia, I was already trying to figure out how to off myself. It was horrible."

Jake's jaw dropped. "What do you mean you *died* of hypothermia?"

"That's what I mean... I *died* of hypothermia. Claire found me walking in the snow. She brought me here."

Jake looked at Claire, and she gave him a sad smile and looked away. Jake looked back at Daniel. "What is going on, Daniel?"

"You did everything to help me, Jake. Thank you so much for that. You even put your life on the line for me. I'm really sorry you..."

Jake shook his head. "Really sorry I what? Daniel? Tell me."

Daniel sighed. "Jake... you died. Claire told me she found your body in a cave. You died of pneumonia. I'm... I'm sorry, Jake."

Jake gasped and wanted to cry, but no tears came out. He looked around the living room. He watched as the dead danced slowly with smiles on their faces to Nat's sweet and lovely voice. Some people were at the food table, chatting and eating. Claire had come down and talked to the guy that Jake noted as a hipster.

Christmas in the Empty Cabin

Jake turned back around to Daniel. "It's Christmas?"

Daniel nodded solemnly.

"Jesus Christ, Daniel. How long have we been... dead?"

"You... two days. Me, one."

A tear dripped down Jake's face. "What about Sheryl and Phillip? Oh... oh no, this isn't happening." Jake held his head and walked around in a small circle.

"Jake, there was nothing you could do about it. You died a hero and a true friend. You did all you could. Claire told me that they had already got the news about... us. A search team had already found our bodies. Let them grieve first, Jake. Then you could go see them once the smoke clears, okay?"

Jake put a hand to his head. "I could do that?"

"Yes. Just talk to Claire about it. She knows a lot about what's going on here." Daniel pulled up his pants leg. "Look, no more broken ankle. And I'm not dying from hypothermia—no cold. I feel... great."

Jake saw that. He also didn't feel any ounce of pain or sickness. He looked at the Christmas tree and then back at Daniel. "What do we do now?"

"We enjoy ourselves. It's Christmas. Let's take it one step at a time, okay?"

Jake nodded his head.

"Let's go meet these folks."

From the outside, the empty cabin was dark and empty. But to clairvoyant people—or wolves—the house was lit with Christmas lights and had music playing and people laughing and talking. The chimney threw smoke into the winter air, but only those with a gift could see it. And although death had taken the mortal lives of everyone at the party, it was still a wonderful Christmas time in the empty cabin.

A SCURRY FURRY CHRISTMAS

1

It was Christmas Eve, and as soon as I drove into the shopping plaza known as the Desert Pavilion, I saw the hordes of cars coming in and out like some metallic centipede. The license plates I saw came in different variations: some from locals (Arizona), some from Sonora, Mexico, Utah, Washington, and Oregon.

"Oregon?" I frowned in disgust. "Why in the hell would you leave Oregon for *this* city?" I received no answer because I was driving alone.

Why would I take my wife and daughter to Rupert's?

Rupert's was a leading department store. They carried clothing, electronics, the ever-popular Buckstar Coffee, toys, music, movies, food, and everything except guns and ammunition. You can get guns at the other store where people shop in unkempt pajamas and bras.

E. Reyes

This store was hip and fun for shoppers, but it was a pain in the neck if you were employed there. I was a grocery stocker and; I guess you can say, the caretaker for the bakery and produce items Rupert's carried. I was the god who would cast away the bad apples (literally) and bring new ones to the table to bake under the bright lights.

As my gaze returned to the cars driving out and driving in the Desert Pavilion, I saw a beat-up beige truck with a big, round, red nose on the grill and one antler clinging on to dear life on the roof. The driver was wearing a red hat with a quote I didn't care to read. One of those ugly trucker hats that greets many lot lizards in rural truck stops around America. The Red Hat spat a wad of brown juice out of his window. He honked at a person before him and called him a cuck.

In another car, I could have sworn it was Kim Kardashian driving. But as I got closer, I was wrong. It was a Mexican woman probably kicking fifty's door down, and her face was pounded and slapped with gobs of makeup. Her lips almost looked like tiny, swollen bratwursts, ready to burst. Her cheekbones resembled a fighter's who took one hell of a beating, and her nose was a thin and frail thing that was contoured heavily. Her cartoonish breasts were smashed against the steering wheel. She had probably already lost consciousness due to a lack of air. She had the visor flipped down, applying mascara to the gigantic lashes on her eyes that resembled Venus flytraps—while driving! She had a teenage boy in the passenger seat who was zombified by his phone, rocking those headphones that didn't have a wire.

I bet a bunch of kids want those; I thought. And then I remembered what my daughter Tina had asked me two weeks ago: "Um, daddy, um, can I ask Santa for a Scurry Furry? That is all I want."

Tina is eight years old. She is a shy, timid, intelligent, and observant girl—the total opposite of my clumsiness and awkwardness. And one of the many great traits that my daughter has is being unselfish. Every Christmas, since she could talk, she always asked for one thing and one thing only. Her mother and I didn't suggest she do that. She just started that tradition of hers on her own.

So, two weeks before, I told her I would get her a Scurry Furry even if I had to fight off angry mothers and flippers who'd sell the damn things online for quadruple the price. They were going to be no match for daddy. I was going to get my hands on that plush even if I had to put my hands on someone. Just kidding.

I found a convenient parking space and thanked the gods for that one. As I rushed across the street, I was nearly struck by a car playing a popular Ariana Grande song loudly. I took a look at the driver. It was a man-child who was wearing oversized cubic zirconia earrings. His hair looked like all the other teens: sideshow-bobbish with a bit of Jonah Hill from *Superbad*. He took a puff of his vape pen and flipped me off. I had no time for him, so I just prayed that his vape pen exploded in his face. Cruel, I know. I ran inside the store, nearly knocking over a girl taking a selfie with an old man dressed as an elf.

2

The store was packed. You'd think Keanu Reeves showed up blessing the ill and holding a cat. The checkout lanes made me frown and make faces that probably made me look like a maniac. I sighed deeply and headed to clock in, avoiding my team leaders and associates. No small talk that day! Thank you very much.

After clocking in, I zipped through the break room to head out toward the grocery side of the store when I noticed the sad and tired faces of the cashiers and of the women who worked in the style apartment. Their heads were down as they ate their microwave dinners and stared at their phones. It was as if they were forcing themselves to eat something to have more energy to work. If any elf ever told you they had it the worst working for a fat man that likes to eat tons of cookies and drink cow-tit juice like it was going out of style, show them the break room of a department store.

Jesus, I almost said out loud. They all looked like they dropped their pizza face down on the floor.

Before I went to the produce section to start my bruised fruit and vegetable smiting, I had to check if the Scurry Furries were still there. A Scurry Furry is a six-inch ball of yellow bird-like hair with big black eyes, a wide razor-sharp smile, blue-ish duck-like legs, and feet, and it said things like "Hungry!" and "Hehehe!" when you squeezed it.

I had come face to face with the toy aisle, and my anxiety crippled me. The section was as crowded as a Beyonce concert. Was she here? I thought. Was Queen Bey here? Who was here? Why were there so many people here? Is online shopping not a thing anymore? Why did everybody wait until the last minute?

So did you, I thought to myself.

Shut up! I replied.

Christmas in the Empty Cabin

I squeezed into the crowd and feared that somebody would start a mosh pit at any moment. I did not want to catch a bony elbow in the face from a grandma, so I hurried to the Scurry Furry section.

They were all gone.

My heart dropped. Sweat poured.

I suddenly felt faint.

I was going to puke the pizza I had eaten for lunch on somebody, and then fall with all my dead weight on some poor unsuspecting child gazing at a Batman figure. He looked up at me for a second, almost as if he knew.

I gathered myself, took a deep breath, calmed my nerves, and scanned the people around me. None of them were holding a Scurry Furry. Rupert's had received a shipment that morning (I asked and asked when they were coming in), meaning they sold out as soon as the doors had opened.

Why couldn't they all buy a tickle-me Elmo or a Turbo Man doll? Leave the Scurry Furries alone!

3

The rest of my work shift was horrendous. People were rude to me, calling me "Rupert's guy" repeatedly, and I started grinding my teeth each time I heard it. When I was busy putting pizza boxes into the coolers, an old lady hit me with her shopping cart—purposely. It was a tight space, so I guess it was her way or the highway. A kid kicked a soccer ball into my groin and ran away.

I had to cashier because the checkout lines got too hectic. I had to deal with a rude young lady who wanted to ad-match KY Jelly, but couldn't because it was against our policy. And to make it worse, her mother then proceeded to ask me which jelly I thought worked best. It was just a miserable time.

When it was time to return to the grocery department, I was relieved.

A lady approached me as I took out some outdated cheese and replaced it with new packages.

"Excuse me," she said, gazing at my clothes and work badge, "do you work here?"

I didn't do it on purpose, but out of reaction to such a rhetorical question, I took a look at my Rupert's badge. Then I looked down at my red Rupert's shirt and stopped to look at the handheld device in my hand to defect the cheese. I gazed at the cart next to me that only Rupert's employees used, filled with go-backs from other aisles. I so badly wanted to say, No. I just love to wear Rupert's colors. I made my own badge—see? I stole this cart from an actual employee, took his scanning device, ran into their backroom, got some cheese, and now I'm going to stock this and fix it all up for free! This is what I do in my free time. But anyway, may I help you, ma'am?

But instead, I kindly said yes and showed her where Preparation H was.

A few minutes later, I heard over the walkie that there were three boxes of Scurry Furries in the back, and they would bring them out.

Fuck! I have to get one, I thought. I had to go back to the toy aisle.

As if someone read my mind, Sandy—the team lead that night—called me on the walkie-talkie as I set some cans of whipped cream in the cooler. People were buying this stuff like cocaine, so I had to ensure it was overstocked.

Christmas in the Empty Cabin

"Tom? Tom from grocery?"

I rolled my eyes and clicked the mic button. "Yes, Sandy?"

"Can you assist Frank in the toy aisle, please? He has a huge crowd, and they're getting out of hand. Security was up there, but they had already apprehended two people and taken them to the back to wait for the police. I guess a woman bit another woman for one of those ugly duck things."

"Scurry Furries? The chicks from Hell?"

Sandy ignored me. "Can you go help him, please?"

"Sure. On my way." I had placed the last can of whipped cream in the cooler. I put aside my fast mover and headed over to the toy aisle.

4

Before I walked up, I could already hear the screams and shouts from customers as they insulted each other over Scurry Furries. I couldn't believe my ears. Nobody should be called a fuck-ass or a whore over some popular toys.

Poor Frank was in the middle of the madness, trying to bring the tension down. But telling an angry and hysterical Christmas shopping crowd to calm down was like washing your car on a rainy day: pointless and stupid.

"Would you all calm down for a sec? Jesus! Like a bunch of damn animals!" said Frank. The tendons in his neck were strained, and his face was red with anxiety. Beads of sweat surrounded his abnormally shiny bald head. My co-workers and I once joked that he puts a bowling ball shine on it.

The crowd was not listening to Frank. Three people played tug of war with boxes of Scurry Furries that were beaten. I was glad that none of them were the open-carry-type men because we would have had worse problems.

Right before me, an old Mexican lady shot out of the crowd and landed on her ass. She made a loud *woof!* after hitting the floor. An older woman wearing athletic gear and a Devil's Hill University hat hugged a Scurry Furry box.

"It's mine, you old hag!" said the athletic woman. She was staring down at the old woman with anger and a crazy look in her eyes that could penetrate any target with fear. I had barely stepped into the crossfire of her stare and admittedly was scared for my life.

I helped the old lady up. She told me "Thank you" in Spanish and fixed the black shawl she was wearing. Not to be mean or anything, but the woman reminded me of a witch who wore an unhealthy and revolting amount of Avon perfume. She was about five-one, had black, scraggly hair, a long nose, a big, brown mole on her cheek, and she was dressed in all black, like Marilyn Manson.

The old woman pointed a twisted and bony finger at the woman and said something in Spanish. She uttered something with disgust and spat on the floor. The crowd around us recoiled, and they were finally silent, ready to spectate. A few people started recording the scene on their phones.

"The cart attendant is getting that one," said Frank, gazing at the wad of spit on the floor. He shook his head.

The old woman then looked at the crowd and said something else that didn't sound like "Merry

Christmas and Happy New Year." She cocked back some phlegm and spit again.

"Yup. Cart attendant is definitely cleaning this shit," said Frank.

The old woman smiled—she smiled at us all. She gave every one of us in that toy aisle her attention. Her beady black eyes and wrinkled smile were scary. After she was done, she said adios and walked away.

"What was that all about?" said the athletic woman.

"Um, you pissed her off after you knocked her on the floor and took the damn Scurry Furry would be my guess," I said. I couldn't help myself.

This was when everything escalated quickly.

5

As Frank asked the athletic woman something, I noticed that the Scurry Furry in the box was shaking a little. Its feathery yellow body was twitching and convulsing.

I looked toward the other customers still holding onto the Scurry Furry boxes, and they had their eyes on Frank and the woman. I noticed that the Scurry Furries in their boxes were shaking, too.

How do they not feel that? I thought. I didn't remember seeing if those toys shook or vibrated. I just saw how they could peel back those black oily lips and smile with those razor-sharp-looking teeth on display. And the way they talked in their chipmunk-style voice.

I was about to say something about the Scurry Furries when I noticed they started blinking those black eyes, but it was too late. The Scurry Furry that the athletic woman held in her arm opened its mouth and bit through the plastic screen of the box. Then it bit down on her forearm, sending a spray of blood all over Frank's face and onto the floor.

"Gaaaaahhh!" the woman let out.

The Furry gnawing on her arm made a maniacal giggle as it bit and chewed the woman's flesh.

The crowd screamed and started running in every direction like roaches. But the two shoppers still stubbornly clung to the Scurry Furry boxes.

People pushed past me and moved around me, but I was stuck in shock, watching as an ugly-cute thing was staining its yellow furry face with human blood. Its bird-like feet clung to the woman's wrist as it continued to eat its meal.

Frank grabbed the Furry and roared as he attempted to pull the little fucker off the woman's arm. The woman screamed louder, but Frank didn't see why.

As Frank yanked the Furry up, holding it as it wiggled around, it had the woman's median nerve and artery in its teeth. They were stretching like a gory Armstrong doll. The vein severed, spraying more blood—some landing on my shoe, and the woman fainted—collapsing on the floor.

Frank saw the horror spilling from the woman's forearm and got weak in the knees.

I called for him. "Frank! Stay with me, man. Stay—"

Frank's eyes rolled back, showing only the whites, and he uttered something that sounded like "Fuck me" before collapsing.

His arms and hands went slack as he hit the floor, and that was when the Furry came loose. The thing looked at me with its intelligent eyes and grimaced.

Christmas in the Empty Cabin

Something like a yelp escaped my mouth when we both locked eyes. The Furry turned around, hopping on its skinny legs, and pounced on Frank. It ran up his belly, dashed between his man boobs, opened its mouth, and landed on his neck.

I turned away before seeing more human anatomy on display. But I could hear squishy sounds, pops here and there, and that high-pitched laughter that the Furry made as it devoured my co-worker in a frenzy.

6

When I looked up from the two dead people before me, I saw that I was still the only one in the toy aisle. I saw people running in the main aisle as screams and cries rang throughout Rupert's.

The Furry on Frank's neck stopped munching and hopped around to face me. Without hesitation, I ran to the little thing and kicked the fucker in the face. The thing squealed like a demonic pig as my foot launched the creature into the air. I punted the Furry so hard that it hit the tall ceiling, breaking it directly on one of the lights.

Pop! went the light as the Furry smashed into it. Sparks exploded from the beam. The thing was executed without a doubt, but I didn't stand around to see, because pieces of glass were raining down. The Scurry Furry fell from the ceiling in a small smoking heap of black fur and landed on Frank's face.

I ran out of the aisle and saw the two shoppers holding the Furry boxes dead on the floor. One was hanging over a new movie display, and the other was lying dead under a pile of Taylor Swift vinyl albums.

I heard screaming and looked up.

A Scurry Furry was chasing a big man, and he started to wail like a girl once he saw the thing running after him. He was screaming the way my daughter did whenever a fly got too close to her, which was very horror-movie-like.

"Fucking save me! Fucking save me!" the man pleaded.

A girl named Rita, who worked in Electronics, ran to his rescue and called me a pussy as she brushed against me. Her light brown shoulder-length hair bounced and flew as she ran like some champion sprinter.

"Huh?" I said to her. I wasn't being a pussy—I was just in shock. And if the circumstances were different, switch the live Scurry Furry with a chihuahua—then I would have laughed my ass off at the big man being chased. I kinda wanted to laugh at that moment, but the shock of everything happening was subduing it, thankfully.

Rita was wielding a baseball bat, and she was chasing the Furry.

"Pleeeeease!" the man screamed. He tripped over a plastic Santa statue and fell over.

The Scurry Furry hopped up, ready to pounce, and then Rita swung and hit the thing with full force. It was like being a kid again and watching the juiced-up McGwire hit those homers.

The Scurry Furry exploded in a ball of yellow feathers and black, slimy blood.

Rita gagged and dropped the baseball bat.

"Ohmygod. That smells like a fart," she said with a hand covering her mouth. She gagged again. "Ohmygod, it stinks so bad."

The big man got up, wiping tears from his eyes. "Thank you so much, ma'am. I—I—Gees, I thought I was a goner!" He started crying hard and placed his face on Rita's shoulder, covered in the Furry's weird blood.

The big man looked up from her shoulder and frowned, sobbing. "It did smell like a fart. Weird."

Rita looked back at me and shook her head.

And then it occurred to me that there was still one more Scurry Furry terrorizing the customers.

"Shit, there's still one more!" I said to Rita.

"You go get it, Tom. I don't get paid enough for this shit."

I scoffed. "Shit, neither do I, Rita!"

I ran to the left, hearing the screams coming from the front of the store. I had to do something.

"Wait!" said Rita.

I turned back and saw that she had gently moved the big man off her shoulder. He covered his face in his meaty palms and continued crying. She bent down and picked the baseball bat up with her index and thumb fingers, doing so like a crab. Black slime dripped from the business end.

"You might wanna take this."

I shook my head. "I ain't touching that shit."

"Well, go fuck yourself, Tom!" She dropped the bat.

I frowned and grabbed a shopping cart.

7

When I got to the main aisle before the checkout, I saw the Scurry Furry in the makeup section. It was hopping on the shelves and crashing into mascaras. I even saw the little fucker kicking stuff off shelves as a cat would have.

A little girl watched in horror as the Scurry Furry bounced around and laughed like a demonic chipmunk. She shook her head, holding in a cry. "I don't want one of those for Christmas anymore," she said.

Hearing her voice, the Furry turned around and hissed. It hopped down from the shelves and started running toward the girl.

The girl screamed as she saw the toy she had wanted so badly start to chase her.

"Don't you dare, Scurry Furry! Don't you dare!" I screamed at it, but it paid me no mind.

The little critter had already tasted human flesh because its mouth was splashed with gore, and it wanted more.

I pushed the cart and started my chase.

The little girl started running toward the exit.

She slipped and nearly lost balance.

"Shit!" I said aloud. I did not want to see a little girl be eaten and killed by some freak toy.

The girl hit a right and was gunning for the exit doors.

"Go! Run out!" I told her.

I was right behind the Furry. The little thing was running as fast as the little girl was.

The little girl slipped over a Buckstar Coffee napkin right before the exit, and that was it. The Scurry Furry pounced.

8

Well, I thought it was it, but it wasn't. The girl slipped on the napkin, but then she caught her balance and pushed through the exit doors. A crowd of people was already out there.

The Scurry Furry was right behind, and so was I with the shopping cart.

People screamed as they saw the Furry emerge. Someone snapped a picture with the flash on, which gave me the advantage.

The Scurry Furry shrieked, blinded by the light, and that was when I charged faster and ran the thing over with the shopping cart's wheel.

Splat!

Black goo exploded on the ground and on my shoes. The smell of rotting ass immediately drifted from the thing's body.

A man came running up.

"Excuse me!" he said. "Do you guys have any more Scurry Furries?"

I laughed. "Well, there's one right here." I pointed to the black and yellow feathery gunk on the ground.

I had to stay for about two hours after everything went down. A couple of witnesses from the toy aisle and I had explained to some men-in-black-like men that we believed a witchy woman put a spell on the toys, but they told us to shut up and never speak of it again. We had to sign some contracts, change our story as a collective, and were promised a handsome amount of cash as long as we cooperated with the agreement.

If we were to go on record or a podcast talking about the incident that really happened, which was so not a rabid dog scare, we would meet fatal measures. So I told them I valued my life, said thanks for the cash, handed over my bank account and routing number, and went home.

It was Christmas Eve, and I wanted to be with my family.

On my way home, the traffic was still crazy. People honked in rage at each other, waved their hands out of their car windows, and flipped the bird, all while listening to Christmas music. I found it wildly entertaining and hilarious to be wanting to beat the hell out of a total stranger while "Last Christmas" by Wham! was playing loudly in the car. I should have been the one flipping out like these animals. I had to kill Scurry Furries earlier that day!

I finally got to my apartment and sat in the parking lot for a while. The sketchy government guys gave us new clothes, so I opted for an ugly Deadpool Christmas sweater. I also grabbed some expensive jeans and killer boots that Rupert's carried. I was glad not to be covered in Scurry Furry blood and smelling like a dead ass.

I had to clear my head.

I was told that I couldn't tell my wife about the incident, so I told her that somebody had called out, so I had to stay a little later. The government hush money would back up my story, anyway.

I stepped out of my car and let the crisp and cold winter air envelop me. I breathed in deeply and enjoyed the aroma of chimneys burning. I also smelled ovens roasting turkeys and hams and wished I could smell red chile beef tamales.

As I walked up to my apartment with its beautiful Christmas lights and garland wrapped around the windows and wood beams, I couldn't help but feel

Christmas in the Empty Cabin

thankful and happy that I was home. That the two people that I loved most in the world were there, inside.

I was finally home. It was a transition from the brightly lit fluorescent store with maniacs running wild. Not to mention the things that I would never talk about again.

What would I tell my daughter on Christmas morning when she saw that I didn't get her a Scurry Furry? I thought at the moment. Sure, they couldn't all be possessed, but who knew? I couldn't take my chances. And if I had to see another one of those fucking things, I'd probably scream.

I shook my head and cleared my mind again.

I imagined my wife and daughter laughing and smiling. Having a good time as *Home Alone* or *A Christmas Story* played in that same infinite loop it does around Christmastime. I could already smell the scent of the sweet honey-glazed ham coming from our home. This was Christmas, my family.

I approached the doorstep and stopped.

A small box with a red silk bow and a shipping label was right by the door. I picked it up and read that it was to my wife, from Rupert's.

Curious about what was in the box, I grabbed my boxcutter from my pants pocket and slit the box open.

I gasped in shock and covered the box back up immediately.

What had been staring at me with its big black eyes and devilish smile behind a plastic screen was a Scurry Furry.

I turned away from my front door, held the box in front of me, and kicked the fucking thing into the sky. It landed on the street.

A big and tall truck that was certainly compensating for something came speeding. The truck's ginormous tires smashed the box flat and roared away.

I smiled. I was relieved. "Merry Christmas, you Scurry fuckin' Furry."

I turned around and went to my family.

AFTERWORD

I want to thank everyone who has helped me with my writing, shared my books, and interacted with me whenever I pop up on social media.

Thank you all for allowing me to share my stories with you. And thank you all for being patient with my re-edits and grammatical headache-inducing errors. I polished my work and finally felt happy, proud, and confident in my stories. And as cliche as it sounds, it would have never been possible without you, the reader.

I hope you enjoyed *Christmas in the Empty Cabin and other Holiday Tales.* And if this is your second time reading these stories, I hope they are much better to read now.

E. Reyes
November 1st, 2020
Tucson, Arizona

ABOUT THE AUTHOR

E. Reyes is a writer, a horror fanatic, and the author of the novel *The House on Moon Creek Avenue.*

Overloading on books and movies and working retail, Reyes brings terror and the unimaginable to everyday life with his experiences and transcends them into a different range of characters and situations.

When not watching scary movies and reading books, E. Reyes is busy being a father and a husband and putting in time playing Xbox. He resides in Arizona.

Printed in Great Britain
by Amazon